Adventures of Kiki Smart Book

Aneala Lance

ARPress
45 Dan Road Suite 5
Canton MA 02021

Hotline: 1(800) 220-7660
Fax: 1(855) 752-6001

Ordering Information:
Quantity sales. Special discounts are available on quantity purchases by corporations,
associations, and others. For details, contact the publisher at the address above.

Printed in the United States of America.

ISBN-13:   Paperback   979-8-89389-913-9
            eBook   979-8-89389-915-3
            Hardback   979-8-89389-914-6

Library of Congress Control Number: 2024923909

Before she can protect children and their families Kiki Smart seeks advice from Jesus and asks for His anointing and Guidance. She seeks daily guidance through prayer and the reading of Gods' word thanking Jesus for saving her, cleansing her and filling her with His Holy spirit. Kiki Smart also prays for children that are all around the world and those children who are sick and suffering she prays for their strength and for them to get better and that Jesus blood will make them better.

Kiki Smart is only smart because of her anointing through Jesus Christ as she yields to him and encourages young children to worship God and go to Sunday school and church as a whole. She encourages them that Jesus Loves all the little children. She encourages all children around the globe to pray to Jesus for he is a help in the present time which we all live. Now I lay me down to sleep I pray the Lord My soul to keep if I should die before I wake, I pray the Lord my soul to take.

Mathew 19:14

But Jesus said, "Let the children alone, and do not hinder them from coming to Me; for the kingdom of heaven belongs to such as these."

New American Standard Bible

HOLY
BIBLE

Look up in the sky its' a dove its' an Angel almost no its' Kiki smart flying under the anointing with the Grace,Mercy and Peace from our Lord and savior Jesus Christ protecting our children while their parents are sleeping, working and knitting. She flies and protects our children with the power given unto her from Christ. Flying with the anointing dropping it upon the earth to all children and their families that they might be well and safe and glorify the Lord in Heaven.

Isaiah 11:6

"A little child shall lead them."

Children do not be of Bullies there is a way out tell your parents, teachers, or truancy officers if you are being bullied and picked on. Kiki smart does not like bullies either, this bully tried to take a child's milk. Kiki Smart was flying around in the area. She saw what had happened and taught this bully a lesson because Mike told that the bully had taken his milk and the bully would not give it back so Kiki Smart fought the bully, bully hit Kiki first and through the power of God she fought him back and beat him up and returned meke his carton of milk. She informed the children on the bus to please let teachers and parents know when they are being bullied. Parents tell your children the story of Daniel in the lion's Den, because when they are being bullied that is what it feels like. Pray for them that God will deliver them to out of the mouth of bullies.

A Prayer for Help from Bullies

Lord as I am in school or wherever bullies may be, please protect me and guide me. For I am afraid I even pray for the bully that he would leave me alone and be nice to other children. Please show the bullies that it is not nice to pick on children. Give me the strength to stand up for myself with you Lord standing up in me and protecting me. Give me the wisdom every day on how to deal with bullies when they bother me and shut the mouth of the bully like you did the lion when Daniel was in the lion's den. I trust you will do the same for me Lord Jesus I trust and thank you for what you are going to do Lord, please help all children with bullying issues like me Amen.

Daniel 6:22

"My God sent his angel, and he shut the mouths of the lions.
They have not hurt me, because I was found innocent in his sight.
Nor have I ever done any wrong before you, Your Majesty."

SCHOOL
BAM!
BULLY
POW

Children I hate the Covid19 too, but with proper handwashing and eating right we can kill that old germ, that virus called Covid19. All we have to do is take our vitamins and practice safe and frequent handwashing. Talk to your parents and teachers on other ways of fighting Covid19. Meanwhile continue to meet teachers and health educators for a prosperous journey in learning. Remember to practice social distancing by staying 6 feet apart from everyone whenever outdoors. Remember to wear masks at all times and gloves when necessary, practice frequent handwashing and hand sanitizing. Also keep hands away from face and mouth. Follow instructions from health care providers, parents, or caregivers for future avoidance of Covid19. Remember kids we are the future remember that song by Whitney Houston I believe The Children are The Future? Well kids we are no matter what may come or what happens we are the future. Let me Kiki Smart take care of the Covid19 by beating it to death.

Children do not be afraid of COVID19.

Here are some helpful Tips to fight COVID19.

1. Wash hands frequently
2. Do not touch face or mouth
3. Take vitamin C and the vitamins doctors give you.
4. Make sure you see your doctor as scheduled.
5. Listen to your doctor.
6. Take all medicines doctors prescribed.
7. Listen to your parents.
8. Take naps and rest well.
9. Say your prayers always.
10. Eat healthy your vegetables.

Follow these rules children and I will help fight Covid19 with you

Jeremiah 33:6

"Nevertheless, I will bring health and healing to it; I will heal my people and will let them enjoy abundant peace and security"

STOP
718-673-0081
Office location:
SHeeping Tm
RUNS
QUEENS ON
TH
BOOM!
POW

Children are a masterpiece
Cut with a special design
They ask amazing questions
So, their brain can fall in line
Children of tomorrow
There past becomes today
As they glean and learn their future
Letting nothing get in their way
Why does it rain
Why is the sky blue?
So many questions to answer
To the children this is all brand new
From the ugly duckling
To mother goose
The questions they ask
Answers we must loose
Whitney said children are the future
Those words came in a song
Children are masterpieces
The future is where they belong
Children are a blessing
Ordained and anointed
Chosen by God
They will be appointed

I know that schoolwork can be frustrating that is why I am creating some tutorials for you which includes math, reading and English help I am working on it now. However, Mary could not wait she needed hands on experience with some schoolwork, so I took it upon myself to help her even though she was a little frustrated we worked together and solved some math equations. She worked hard and I was able to show her some formulas to help with problem solving. You too can get the help you need in this season to overcome math, reading and English. I know in this season because of the Covid19 we are working on the computers with teachers and educators to go to the next level in learning. Kids I promise you I will get those tutorials out to you as soon as possible. Mary has passed her math exam I was so honored to be able to assist her in her learning efforts. Keep up the good work Mary see ya soon!

Exodus 31:3

"And I have filled him with the Spirit of God, with ability and intelligence, with knowledge and all craftmanship"

MATHEMATICS
LI
12

At last I am honored to go before Prince Harry and Princess Megan to talk about our children all around the globe. I wanted to talk to them about ways of beating the Covid19 and how I could assist them. The Prince and his wife were very much concerned about the children all around the world. He expressed to me that him and the princess had just left Africa and had made sure the medical supplies lots of food and water were given to children over there. I was pleased to hear that a lot of my concern is for not just the children in America, but the children in 3rd world countries. I told the Prince and Princess to let me know when they would be headed back to Africa because I would like to be a part of their I told them that I could help with medical supplies food, school supplies and water next journey. They explained to me that they were headed to Bangladesh and from there they would be going to Israel.

I told them I could assist with school supplies medical supplies food and water and that I would get it to them as quickly as possible. They agreed it was a good idea and asked if I could come, I told them next time because I had to meet with the President of the United States Donald Trump. I told them to have a safe Journey and that I would be praying for them. They hugged me and we said farewell to each other. Thank you, Prince Harry and Princess Megan, if Princess Diana were here, she would be proud of both of you I said, have a safe journey.

Proverbs 18:16

"A man's gift opens doors for him and brings him before great men."

I had to bust through the doors of the white house. Entering through the doors was not going to do it. I had to make my presence known by coming through the walls. Now Children I was not happy with the speech our president was making so I asked him for once in his life to tell the truth and to it for the kids. I had my hands folded and was upset with our president because of his lies. I told him that the majority of the people in America were tired of him lying all the time and that he needs to make peace by telling the truth. I am heartbroken that many people died so many children lost parents, I asked our president how would he feel if he were a child and he lost his parents or could not go to school because of this terrible virus. All he could do was look at me in despair. He said who are you I said my name is Kiki smart and I represent the children around the globe. Do not destroy our future for we are the future, and I will not allow you to destroy us. Now you get it together Mr. Trump or God Himself will deal with you shortly and everything that is connected to you. I decree and Declare that the people all around the Globe will live in the Name of My Lord and savior Jesus Christ I stamp this declaration with the blood of Jesus. Line up with the will of God Mr. President or be gone out of office. Goodbye Mr. President.

Titus 1:13

"This testimony is true. Therefore, rebuke them sternly,
so that they will be sound in the faith".

THE WHITE HOUSE
WASHINGTON

Oh well kids it was very nice meeting you all I hope you enjoyed this book as I enjoyed speaking to you. Time to go to church with my grandmother her name is Aneala Lance she is known as Dr. Lance. I call her Grandma Nela she is the one who teaches me about God. I go to church with her on Sundays. On Sundays we are on the zoom conference line 929-205-6099 pin is 2798272024.Now if you want to join us live we are at https// us02web.zoom.us/j/2798272024. I hope this was helpful I now have to go to church with my grandmother do not forget the prayer line numbers call in Apostle Lenabelle Carr is pastor of this church a true Prayer warrior. God Answers prayer I would not be who I am today if It was not for prayer. Remember Children I am praying for you always.

Proverbs 22:6

*Train up a child in the way he should go; even when
he is old, he will not depart from it.*